I0527186

Hattie Leonard Wright

At the twilight hour and other poems

Hattie Leonard Wright

At the twilight hour and other poems

ISBN/EAN: 9783337124632

Printed in Europe, USA, Canada, Australia, Japan

Cover: Foto ©Andreas Hilbeck / pixelio.de

More available books at **www.hansebooks.com**

At The Twilight Hour

and

OTHER POEMS

BY

HATTIE LEONARD WRIGHT

COPYRIGHT BY
HATTIE LEONARD WRIGHT
1897

CONTENTS

iii

CONTENTS.

Sometimes I sang because the way seemed dreary,
    Sometimes for joy my harp began to thrill.
Sometimes, when Grief stood mute 'neath sorrow weary
    A dirge unlocked her lips so still
And so, through life, my harp and I together
    Have climbed the mountain or have crossed the plain,
It brightened for me all the gloomy weather
    Or soothed some fellow wand'rer's pain.
This little book shall voice some faint vibration
    Of all that thrilled my wand'ring harp of yore,
As some small shell of ocean's strange creation
    Still sings though wave shall kiss it nevermore.

AT THE TWILIGHT HOUR.

THE last few rays of the fading light
Look back on the earth in ling'ring goodnight,
And the purpling tints of the evening mark
That peaceful time "'twixt daylight and dark"
My happiest time; 'tis the twilight hour.

The soft red glow from the fire-place falls
In flickering gleams athwart the walls,
On table and books and old time chairs,
On quaint old vases marshalled in pairs,
That show through the dusk of the twilight hour.

And, side by side in the fireside glow,
One stately and tall, one little and low,
Two easy chairs invitingly wait,
While I softly whisper, "It's getting late"
In fear we may miss our twilight hour.

But a well-known step's on the flags outside,
A moment later and you're at my side;
Then what do we care for the world without,
For it's praise or blame, for it's faith or doubt?
They vex us not in the twilight hour.

3

Weary and worn from the long day's hard toil,
Brown with the sun, marked with stains of the soil.
Somewhat grizzled and gray, somewhat careworn
    and old,
You are yet more to me than can ever be told
    As we sit side by side in the twilight hour.

The hand that holds mine in clasp tender and
    warm,
Though roughened by toil and scarce graceful
    of form,
Has battled for country in treason's dark hour
And helped to put down rebellion's vile power,
    And I'm proud of it now in this twilight hour.

As we silently sit in the deepening gloom
That gathers and grows in our firelighted room,
I think of the hardships, the sorrow and care
That have furrowed your brow and silvered your
    hair;
    I would make you forget in this twilight hour.

Then I think of the years that are yet to be,
Bearing bitter and sweet for you and for me,
And I know the cup will be sweeter if we
May share it together, whate'er it may be.
    'Tis of this that I dream in this twilight hour.

Oh, I pray when, at last, our tasks are all done
And together we watch life's fast setting sun,
When the tender Angel of Death shall come
Our spirits to bear to our Heavenly Home,
We may rest side by side in that twilight hour.

I GROW.

IN a cleft of a rock both dark and deep
    There fell a seed long ago ;
One glimmering ray broke its wintry sleep
    And woke it to live and grow.
Prisoned from day in the darkness of night,
    Not even a leaflet near,
It pined for the dew and the warmth and light
    And hated the darkness drear.
Far, far overhead shone a glimpse of blue,
    And up from the depths came clear
The sound of a spring that had trickled through
    For many, many a year.
So, because it could not *live* in the dark,
    Because it must drink or die,
It reached forth its leaves to the shining mark
    (That was all it could see of sky);
It sent down a thirsty rootlet to drink
    From the fountain flowing below,
And down in its heart it began to think,
    "I really believe that I grow."

       *   *   *   *

Years came and went and a graceful young tree
    Had reared there its beautiful crest,
And every bright leaf as it fluttered free
    In the wind from the warm southwest

Sang the sweet song that the first time was heard
    In cold, cheerless darkness below.
How happiness thrilled and throbbed in each word
    "I grow, I grow! Oh, I grow!"

      *   *   *   *

Boughs were wrenched off by the furious gale
    Or burnt in the lightning's flame ;
And leaves fell thick 'neath the fast flying hail,
    The song was ever the same.
Heaviest storms spent their fury in vain,
    Droughts parched the earth far and near,
'Mid the thunder's roar came the old refrain
    "I grow, I grow,"—sweet and clear.
And the scars were healed as the years went on,
    Every springtime brought new life,
And flower and fruit crowned the victory won
    Through years of storm and strife.
Still the same old song swelled up to the sky,
    "I grow, I grow! Oh, I grow!"
Till every wind brought the gladsome cry,
    "I grow, I grow! Oh, I grow!"

      *   *   *   *

And so *I* sing through the dreariest night,
    Throughout the weariest day ;
The sun's overhead though clouds keep the light
    From shining across *my* way.
The goal may seem never so far from me,
    The pathway be rough and steep ;

My strength indeed very little may be
    And torrents be wide and deep ;
Tomorrow the sun may shine bright and clear.
    The torrents have ebbed away ;
If not I'll be patient, banish all fear
    And wait yet another day.
And still with a heart full of joy I sing,
    "I grow, I grow ! Oh, I grow !"
There will come, bye-and-bye, a blossoming
    Of life and soul—*this I know.*

SMOKE AND A SERMON.

'TWAS sunset, and, looking across the plain
    And the forest fresh from the recent rain,
I was watching the tender light that lay,
So soft and so bright and so far away,
On the white cloudships that dreamily
Sailed the measureless depths of azure sea.
Toil-smirched and careworn I wished I could be
Clean as a cloud and as buoyant and free ;
My life seemed so gloomy—would it were bright—
But even it's shadow seemed dark'ning to night.
Near by me an engine that stood on the track
Sent skyward a column of smoke thick and black.
Blacker and thicker on upward it rolled
Till the setting sun turned it's top to gold,
Then fair as a cloud, just as softly bright,
It was borne away on the breeze so light.
So, I thought, with life—if we lift it high

It's grimy spots turn to gold in the sky,
If only upon them we catch the ray
Of the Sun that shines through unending Day.
So the inky smoke of our battles may rear
A pillar of cloud in our wilderness here
That shall be as a pillar of light to show
Some wayfaring brother the way to go.

———

MY VIEW AND HIS'N.

I TELL ye jest what, them teachers
  Has 'n awful sight fer ter bear,
An' I couldn't be hired t' be one
  Ef I hadn't a rag t' wear
Except this old suit uv blue-jeans
  An' not nary cent fer t' spare.

Fust, they's a passel uv young uns
  Jest full uv the very Old Nick—
The biggest uns puttin' the littlest
  Up to ev'ry mischeevious trick
An' a keepin' theirselves out uv trouble
  In a way th't seems purty slick.

Then, they's th' intrusted payrents
  Ferever a meddlin' aroun'
An' a faultin' th' teacher fer somethin'
  He knows better 'n they, I'll be boun'.
It hain't possible fer ye ter suit 'em
  Anyways ter suit 'em all roun'.

MY VIEW AND HIS'N.

This one —*he* thinks th't his childern,
    The teacher hain't learned 'em enough,
Th't he's ben by far too easy:
    The next one allows he's too rough:
An' Jones, *hc* says th't he's partial
    An' he's took his'n out in a huff.

An' then, just look at his quarters.
    He boards with th' Widder Van Bloom;
Two mile 'n a half he must foot it
    'Cause th' neighbors here hed'nt room.
Takin' summer 'n winter t'gether
    His comfort it hain't on th' boom.

Fer 'n fall th' roads is so muddy,
    In winter ther drifted with snow,
An' 'n spring th' mud is repeated,
    By June in the dust he must go.
Ef it hain't one thing it's another
    T' make him feel mizzerble low.

Then they's th't dirty old school-house,
    'Tain't fit fer t' stable a cow:
Th' ceilin' all frescoed with spit-balls
    Thet's stuck frum th' fust year tell now,
Th' winders without any curtains,—
    A comfortless place, you'll allow.

They hain't a tree th't stands nigh it
    T' keep off th' blisterin' sun
Th't strikes straight through them old winders

In th' childern's eyes—ev'ry one
Scorchin' an' parchin' an' blindin'
     Tell th' long afternoon is done.

It's jest ez bad in th' winter
     Fer th' glare uv th' dazzlin' snow
Shines through them unshaded winders
     All day with it's pitiless glow :
An' cracks in th' weatherboardin'
     Lets in all th' winds th't blow.

My son, he don't see it thet way ;
     He belives th't teachin's a trade
Much better 'n farmin' or physick
     Or th'n sellin' dress goods 'n braid ;
Th't next to preachin' comes teachin'
     An' th't teachers is born 'n not made.

He says th't them little childern
     Is learnin' *him* some ev'ry day,—
Somethin' he'd either forgotten
     Or th't never come in his way ;
Thet his mind's brighter 'n better
     An' th't thet alone would be pay.

He says th't thet narrer school room
     Is th' big world copied out small,
Where students uv human nacher
     Can find little samples uv all
Th' bodies, brains, dispositions,
     Thet crowd this terrestrial ball.

He says th't th' work uv teachin'
    Is somethin' noble an' grand ;
Thet th' unknown hard-worked teacher
    Today holds fast in his hand
Shapin' fer good er fer evil
    Th' destiny uv our Land.

He says th't it learns him patience
    At th' same time thoroughness
As he tries t' foller th' pattern
    Uv One who will surely bless
Th' work uv th' humblest teacher
    Thet strives in His footsteps t' press.

A LAWYER'S VALENTINE.

AGAIN I rise to greet the day
    That wakens life and feeling,
That brings the songster's sweetest lay,
    His happiness revealing ;
The foremost courier of the May,
    Announcing her in gladness,
The springtime sunshine's earliest ray
    To banish thoughts of sadness.

Full oft I've known the time return,
    Without one fond emotion
To wake this heart, so grave and stern,
    To Love's own sweet devotion.
The fancies fair, that fill the air

THE LAWYER'S VALENTINE.

Upon this happy season,
Could not keep house with heavy care
And stolid sober reason.

But now, a vision floats about
    The must and dust of volumes
And with its presence puts to rout
    My figures in their columns.
A *precedent*, I can't forget,
    Is not the one I've cited,
And gentle *answers* haunt me yet,
    My plea not half indited.

And now, I've written "Valentine"
    Upon the deed I'm framing-
Right in the middle of the line!
    The senior would be blaming
This member of the firm
    Did he but know the courting
That takes my mind this term—
    A suit I'm just reporting.

Dark eyes, that smile above the page,
    With tender timid glances,
Would melt the heart of any flint,
    Or blind a lawyer's senses;
The scarlet lips that tempt my own,
    Their pearly treasures showing,
The lovely brow, a cloud (dark brown)
    Of hair about it blowing;

The echo of a half-breathed "yes,"
    Called "no" the instant after,

Because you would not then confess,
    But fled with mocking laughter;
And, after that, the long, long kiss
    I took, your lips compelling
To yield me all the tenderness
    Denied me in the telling.

I call the vision "Valentine"
    By all the loves of ages -
I call it and I make it mine,
    Recorded in these pages;
And, lest thou doubt my right to do it,
I'll simply sign myself to prove it,
Forever and forever thine—
Thine, and thine only,
                    VALENTINE.

———

JUNE.

OH, the happy, happy time
    When in merry, merry chime,
With sweetly sounding voices
Earth carols and rejoices
To the merry, merry tune
Taught her by the joyful June.

Oh, the joyful, joyful time!
To be sad were now a crime.
Above gay birds are singing,
Below the flowers are springing.

JUNE.

All to deck the golden noon
Of the sunny days of June.

Oh, the quiet, quiet time!
Stillness of a balmy clime.
In languid ease reposing
At daylight's dewy closing.
Guarded by the tender moon.
Dream we of the lovely June.

———

PARTING SONG.

MEM'RY'S wand calls up tonight
The past with all it's shade and light.
Thoughts are with the days of yore—
Oh, happy days, they come no more.
Thinking of the friends they brought.
Rememb'ring all the changes wrought.
Sadness fills each heavy heart.
As now from classmates loved we part.

CHO.—May our lives lead up always,
Illumined by the Sun's bright rays,
Till, surrounded by His light.
Our class shall never say good night.

Let us hope the years gone by
Are but the steps to those on High.
That together there, as here,
All those whom we have held so dear—

PARTING SONG.

Teachers. classmates. one and all.
Not one name missing from the call.
Will have left a mem'ry fraught
With earne-t deeds and loving thought.

Now farewell! Hope doth us show
A flowery path. but who can know
When the rose will show its thorn
How soon the clouds obscure the morn?
One there is. and one alone.
The future can to us make known.
Waiting hearts. bow down in prayer
That God will hold us in His care.

TO A DARWINIAN.

OUT of the protoplasm
    In Chaos' darkest chasm
Went forth two molecules
By evolution's rules.
These, gathering and uniting,—
You see I'm Darwin citing—
With other molecules.
Became two wondrous fools.
And they were. I opine.
You and your valentine.
Now this has quite assured me
That I'm the foolish one for thee
And you're the only fool for me.
So. of two fools. let one fool be.

THANKSGIVING DAY.

TIME waits to gather in today,
  With all his hoarded treasures,
The smiles and tears, the hopes and fears,
  The joys, the griefs, the pleasures,
The prayers, the vows, the prophecies,
The failures and successes,
  The tares and wheat—true grain or cheat
Just as they stood, together,
  That side by side, for many a day
Through fair and darksome weather,
  Have grown and ripened, leaf by leaf,
  To form the year's full rounded sheaf.
And as the Reaper cuts and binds
  The harvest for our sowing
A tricksome fancy round it winds
  A wreath so bright and glowing
Forgetful of the tares and cheat,
Remembering but the golden wheat,
We grieve to find the harvest past
And wish that June could always last.
But, since for us this may not be,
We look upon our sheaf and see
The flowers that hide what's poor and mean,
The grain that looks so fair and clean,
And think that sure no other year
Hath ever brought such rare good cheer.
And so we gather round the board

With Autumn's bounty richly stored,
And quip and jest fly to and fro
    And toasts are drunk and songs are sung.

    *   *   *   *

The dancers range themselves in row,
    The fiddle now is quickly strung,
And to its romping merry tune
    They dance the "Ole Virginny Reel,"
The "Fisher's Hornpipe," "Old Zip Coon,"
    The "double shuffle." (Nimble heel
That takes to dance it well, you see)
    And "Patting Juba,"—all the list
Of fancy steps, from pigeon wings
    To pigeon-*toes.* Each one his best
With all the odd, outlandish flings
    To rouse a rival's jealousy.
The merry games that children know
    Find older players on this day;
And matron staid and grandsire gray
    In "blind man's buff" rush to and fro.
At last around the chimney wide
We draw our chairs close, side by side,
And speak of all those happy days,
Thanksgiving days, that went their ways
Long years ago; of friends that met
    Together here, now gone before;
Of how today we miss them, yet
    We hope to meet them all once more;
Of that glad Day, Thanksgiving Day,
That dawns upon our earthly way
To cheer us as we gently go

Adown the vale to cross the stream
That ripples on the other shore.
  And, while we talk, the fire burns low
With strangely fitful flickering gleam ;
  The shadows lengthen on the floor
Then slowly climb along the wall.
And thoughtful silence wraps us all.
And then the grandsire slowly kneels
And from his place there upward steals,
At first in accents faint with tears
And then in triumph o'er all fears,
A prayer--so full of faith and love
It seems to lift us all above
The clouds that often hide the way
That leads us to Thanksgiving Day.

"THE YEARS GLIDE BY."

THE years glide by, dear friends.
    The years glide by.
Like ripples on a shoreless sea
Where all beyond is mystery
And all behind is memory,
    The years glide by.
And, as our gallant bark, Today,
Sails gaily on her course away,
The years, that never, never stay.
    Glide swiftly by.
Far, far astern a glittering trace
Is all that's left to mark the place

Where our Today passed other days
    As they went by.
And there the glimmering light and shade
Of joy and mirth, bright hopes betrayed,
Show for a moment ; while they fade
    The years glide by.
But, oh, my friends, the years that glide
So swiftly to the farther side- --
    Though they glide *by*
To fade at last in shadowed night,
Come, bright with morning's glorious light,
Bringing us ever new delight,
    As they glide by.
Yet never mourn their speedy flight ;
Because, each tiny moment bright
Speaks of a Land that knows no night,
    Though years glide by.
And surely, though beyond our sight,
For us, if we but steer aright,
"There is a Land of Pure Delight,"
Where the years glide by, dear friends,
    The years glide by.

ARBUTUS.

OH, sweet the warmth of sunny skies,
    Where all things dream in deep repose
And bright the flower that blooms and dies
    Below the belt of frosts and snows !
Kissed by the sun to scarlet hue

It flames in brilliant beauty forth,
And never feels the winds that strew
    The frailer blossoms of the north.
Bathed in the copious dew of night,
    It's color deepens and it goes,
To meet the morning, all bedight
    In deepest tint of velvet rose.
One calls it perfect in its grace,
    The queen of all that bud and bloom.
I never loved an *empty* vase—
    What more's a flower without perfume?
My floweret blooms 'neath colder skies,
    And faint and few are the rays that fall
Where, all snow wrapped, it hidden lies.
    I prize it, though--yes, more than all.
The bleak fall winds and the cold fall rains
    The sunless days and the frosts and snows,
All come and go, while an old year wanes,
    All come and go, while a new year grows.
And, while the earth still in darkness sleeps,
From its bed of leaves my floweret peeps
And shines in its beauty under the snow.
Just tinged with a blush by the winds that blow,
The flower hides away 'neath the leaf's dark green
And buds and blossoms alone, unseen,
While the spring wind bears on it's wings of air
A whiff of an odor both rich and rare;
Faint it may be, till some passing foot,
Strayed from the path, breaks the tender shoot
That yields its sweetest perfume with life.
And so, my sweet, from the turmoil and strife.

From the winds of doubt and the rain of tears,
From the frosts and snows and the grief of years,
You have grown to the perfect, pure, sweet flower
That will live in my heart till it's latest hour.
But frosts must come and skies must lower
And rain must fall, for the perfect flower.
So, bloom the more brightly you will, I know,
For the fairest flowers open under the snow,
And tend'rest hands brush the flakes away
To gather Arbutus' delicate spray.

IN MEMORY OF HELEN NINDE KING.

[One of the sweetest and purest souls that ever blessed this
earth with tender ministrations has passed up higher. And we who
are left are desolate in our bereavement of a life that blessed all
other lives that ever felt its influence.]

SO little time!
    Oh, God, so short the space
To whisper tender, loving words,
    To look upon a precious face!
        So little time!
(Oh, God, how swift it flies)
    To feel the touch of trembling hands
To meet the glance of earnest eyes,
        So little time!
Oh, God, a moment brief
    To feel the kiss of loving lips
On lips all dumb with grief!

IN MEMORIAM.

So little time!
Thank God, the time will be
But brief that we must work alone.
Then time shall be eternity.
A little time,
Thank God, and quickly gone.
Oh, then, why should we grieve?
So soon will our tomorrow dawn.

TO THE MEMORY OF OUR CLASSMATE, JENNIE ARMSTRONG.

WHEN the shades of night are falling,
When our labor's day is done,
We can hear loved voices calling
From the Land beyond the sun.
Ah! One voice has called but lately,
One form we almost can see;
Time has not the vision faded,
Oh, we often think of thee!
Friend, most fortunate of all,
We are left to wait awhile.
"Bide a wee" must we and then
We may meet thy welcome smile.
Can Death break the chain of Friendship?
Can it be that Love has flown?
No! In heaven reuniting
We may claim thee as our own.
Through our tears we read the promise
Fulfilled *there*, but given here.

TO A NOVEMBER VIOLET.

And through sorrow we are slowly
    Upward led, beyond the bier.
Yes, in heaven shall we see thee ;
    Could we hold this promise ever
Brighter would the future shine.
    Now the present seems forever.

———

TO A NOVEMBER VIOLET.

OH Flower of Spring, that lingered here to cheer
    The briefer daylight of a ling'ring fall,
Speak to my darling of another year—
    Of vines that drape an humble cottage wall,
Of birds that build beneath its slanting eaves
    And swing upon the rose-branch at the door ;
Of hope that bourgeons with the budding leaves,
    And Love that waxes more and more.
Smile in her face, my flower, and see thyself
    Reflected in the dark depths of her dusky eyes.
Smile, for the answer of her bending lips
    Shall stir thy beauty with a new, a sweet
        surprise.
Nestle against her cheek, my wee blue flower
    And dream of summer winds and sunny days ;
Breathe in her ear a murmur of that hour
    When last I saw her lovely, flower-like face.
And tell her, oh, my bonny blossom blue,
Tell her, oh, tell her, violets are true ;
Tell her I work and wait for her alone
And tell her, winter will ere long have flown.

TO ISABEL.

A SUMMER'S leaf, that idly sways and falls,
   Mayhap is gathered up and pressed from
      curious eyes away.
Though faded, sere and brown, it still recalls
   The happy days, whose hours did blithely dance,
      forever bright and gay.
So of these hours, that have so quickly passed,
   Remembrance garners up some brighter one and
      hides it safe away
With other reliques of the golden Past.
   And, as around the leaf an odor clings
Redolent of fair days and warm south winds, clover
      and new-mown hay,
   To older years the hour's bright mem'ry brings
A sweeter fragrance still, that scents the inner closets
      of the heart,
   So, round thy pictured face there cluster thick
The forms of those who came and went and in the
      summer play took part ;—
   That play, whose happy scenes passed all too quick!
Then wandering vibrations come to me,
   Echoed from "long ago," to voice this play of
      phantoms from the past.
Ah, that the shades might prove reality
   And each new summer, in delight a repetition
      of the last !
An idle wish—but in the wishing sweet ;
   The play is played the players parted to their
      distant theaters,

Perchance ne'er more upon one stage to meet.
  And other players shall rehearse our play to other
    listeners ;
For others shall the days go happily,
  While other friends shall gather round the board
    where we were welcome guests
And other hands deal hospitality ;
  Upon the boughs, within whose shade we dreamed,
    there will be other nests ;
Our blossoms will for fresher flowers give place.
  But, in the time to come, no time will ever be, no
    friends will seem,
Like by-gone times and friends of other days.
  The fairy forms that fill the fairest dreams
Can not compare with those revealed when memory's
    taper burns
  And shows a happy glimpse of "long ago."
Wherein is but one dark inscription found, and that
    ("It ne'er returns" ,
  Repeated by each year that comes to go
And, in a chorus sad, re-echoed on the borders of
    Today.
  So, as the present soon will be the past.
However pleasant, bright and gay, but momentary in
    its stay,
We'll wish Tomorrow like Today
  And every summer like the last.

———

FALLING LEAVES.

OCTOBER! and a gentle breath
    Comes softly, like the last faint sigh
That parts the lips ere mighty Death

FALLING LEAVES.

Usurps Sleep's throne of mystery.
The south wind blows; how gently now
    It stirs the dying leaves that hang
Their feverish crimson on that bough
    Where once, 'mid springing green, there
      rang
The wild sweet notes of happy birds
    Whose little throats seemed pouring forth
The year's new joy,—too deep for words,
    (For words go halting from their birth.)
The air is filled with leaves that fall
    As pliant tree tops bend before
The breeze that lightly stirs them all
    And piles the rustling heaps with more.
The distance glimmers through a haze
    That wraps it with a veiling charm,
As if to dim the hues that blaze
    From yonder woodland lying warm
Upon the sunny slope that trends
    Full southward, till one scarce may say
If some bright cloud that lowly bends
    Be cloud or mountain far away.

FROM THE PAST.

WITH the ebb tide and flood of the years
    To us both many changes have come.
We have marked them in mirth or in tears
    Day by day as we reckoned their sum.
You are there and I here, and between

FROM THE PAST.

Far, far greater than mile-measured space
Our lives' opposite paths intervene,
  Paths that we ne'er may hope to retrace.
As I muse on the days of my youth
  Oh, how fondly I love to recall,
In their tenderness honor and truth,
  The dear friends that I loved, one and all.
Oh, the amber of mem'ry will hold
  Still embalmed in its own golden glow
These fair wraiths of the glad days of old
  While I live to remember and know.
But I start when some long quiet form
  Is disturbed by a breath from Today
And before me stands living and warm
  When I thought I had laid it away
So securely no sullying stain
  From the grim smoking battle of life
And no throb of life's sorrow or pain
  E'er could reach it and wake it to strife.
Oh, my friend! as you come from my Past
  Thus to enter my Present, I shrink;
For too well do I know that, at last,
  There will shatter or strengthen one link
In the friendships I prized long ago.
  But, when stripped of the graces of Then,
Oh, I wonder shall I surely know
  My old friend when I meet him again
Fully grown to the stature of Now?
  Shall I find stainless honor and truth
Still enthroned, as of yore, on his brow?
  Then thrice welcome, dear friend of my youth.

"NOT HERE, BUT RISEN."

As you pass from my vision again
Stepping back from the *Now* to the *Then*
You will fade to a phantom once more,—
With the shades from the loved haunts of yore
Still illumed by the ambient glow
That aye brightens the dear Long Ago.

———

"NOT HERE, BUT RISEN."

———

[In Memory of Minnie Besley Welles. Died March 24. 1892.]

———

NO, not for her the hue of darkness born ;
 She greets the light of an Eternal Morn.
 Bring not for her the sable badge of
  death
 Who knows but now the joy of
  Heaven's first breath.
 "Not here, but risen," this shall be
 Written for all who come to see.
 Since first beside an open tomb,
 Dispelling all its awful gloom,
 The angel on that glorious day
 Forever rolled the stone away,
 The eye of Faith may ever see
 Not Death but Immortality.
 "Not here, but risen,"—let the white
 Of Easter lilies meet the light,
 So fair and sweet they well may be
 The sign of what we can not see --
 Her life's sweet bud of purity
 Unfolding in Eternity.

THE OLD GRAY HORSE.

A SORRY old nag was the old gray horse,
    With his roughened coat and shaggy mane
And his unclipped locks 'bove his well-worn shoes
    And his knotted tail fringed with frozen rain.
And, as he soberly went on his way
Through the mud and sleet in the morning gray,
Very few, very few would have dared to say
"There was once a time when this old horse gray
"Was a brisk young nag (in the days that are past)
And had even been dubbed, in those early days 'fast.'"
But there had been a time when men shook their
        heads
    And had even declared that the young gray colt.
With his swinging trot at a lightning like pace,
    (Which differed so much from the regular jolt)
Would never do aught excepting to race.
"For an honest day's work," said they, one and all,
"He'll be likely to balk and be sure to stall."
But a patient head and a loving hand
    Were guiding the gray colt's bridle rein ;
    And, although with many a fret and pain,
He learned to know when to stop and to stand.
And little by little he learned the fact
That, to always be able the right to act,
For horses, as well as for men, it is true
A moderate course is the best to pursue.
So, jogging along through the dust or the rain,

Over the hill and over the plain,
When it is wet and when it is dry
The old gray horse goes patiently by,
Carefully plodding where it is rough,
Cheerfully trotting where smooth enough,
Doing his best and doing his all,
Never known to balk, never known to stall.
People may talk with a jeer or a frown
Of his long-haired coat with its mud-stains brown;
May laugh at the quaintly bundled up knot
That nods behind to his regular trot;
But the old gray horse with an unmoved face
Goes quietly by at the same old pace.

EVENING.

DAISIES white are softly blooming,
   Roses sweet are now perfuming
All the air with fragrance rare;
Dew drops pure are clearly shining
Where the vines their leaves are twining
   Evening fair has not a care.

Evening winds are gently blowing;
Patient cows are softly lowing,
   At the gate they stand and wait
For the milkmaid's tardy coming,
Tokened by her distant humming.
   That she's late is due to Fate.

EVENING.

Fate has sent a lover suing
For her hand in earnest wooing.
     Promises of faithfulness
Love and tenderness he pledges,
While the thrush from out the hedges
     Still sings on of love that's gone.

She forgets now that the morrow
Has no certainty but sorrow.
     Present joy has no alloy.
Blythely sings she of her lover
While the birds about her hover,
     Charmed by her tuneful cry.

Maiden, lovers are deceiving,
Birds and flowers will soon be leaving,
     Winter drear will soon be here.
Tend thy kine, so patient waiting
While thy lover is berating
     Time that lags and slowly drags.

All impatient of thy staying,
Of thy long and late delaying,
     Up and down with many a frown
He, with hasty stepping, paces,
Thinking on thy blushing graces.
     Haste to him, the light grows dim.

Twilight all too soon advances,
Robbing him of thy coy glances.
     Mistress calls that darkness falls.

BABY.

Maiden, enter quick thy dwelling,
Never heeding what he's telling
    Of a love that time will prove.

Love tonight's a vesper chiming
In a tender heartfelt timing;
    At each beat it grows more sweet.
But the morrow brings complaining
Of the little love remaining.
    Maiden, all have felt it's thrall.

BABY.

A TINY, grass-grown grave
    Where fern-fronds gently wave
To the music of the rill
Echoed by a distant hill.
The stranger only sees
Stately bending, wind-blown trees
And beneath a tiny mound
Which to him is naught but ground.
That is all: for human eyes
May not see the tears which rise
As the mother calls to mind
Baby fingers that still bind,
Baby ways that still shall charm
While her mother heart is warm.
Baby! Word of matchless grace!
Calling up the rosebud face
Framed in waves of beaten gold,

Dimples, more than can be told,
Grave eyes, in whose azure deeps
A world of thought in silence sleeps.

A POTATOLESS DINNER.

THE Turk lay steaming on the platter.
  The gravy flanked him on the right.
Alas! Whatever was the matter,
  Potatoes—*they* "were out of sight."

And sure, as I'm a living sinner,
  Controlled by some unlucky Fate,
To crown this memorable dinner
  R. M. tipped o'er the gravy plate.

There's one thing sure beyond all question —
  And only one—I'm thankful for,
'Tis that not one from indigestion
  Since left this earthly seat of War.

When next I have a Turk for dinner
  With pumpkin pie and cranberry sauce,
May she grow thin and thin and thinner
  Who makes my *menu* suffer loss.

For if so much as one potato
  Escape the boiling of the pot,
No matter how I really hate to,
  I'll "give it to her" just "red-hot."

CHILDREN'S SONGS.

SONG OF THE SHADOW FAIRIES.

CHILDREN of the leaves and sunshine,
    Blythely dancing all the day,
To the bird-notes thrilling sweetly
    In a measure light and gay;
Ever dancing, dancing, dancing,
    Ever while we may;
Till the dew begins to fall
And the twilight shadows all;
    Then away we fly together
      Till tomorrow brings the sun,
    And the birds again are singing, singing,
      For, till then our play is done.

Tripping o'er the dainty mosses
    Kneeling at a lily's feet;
Chasing after whirling leaflets
    Nodding to the bowing wheat;
Ever dancing, dancing, dancing,
    Still with footsteps fleet;
Kissing many flowers rare,
Floating on the water fair;
    But at dusk we fly together
      To our hidden elfin home
    And await the morrow's coming, coming;
      When the sun shines we may roam.

SONG II.

BIRDIE in the tree-top singing,
  Silv'ry tones around you flinging,
Why are you so bright and gay,
Trilling, chirping, all the day?

Birdie, I do love to hear you
Though I don't dare to come near you.
You're so timid and so shy
When I come away you fly.

Birdie, you do sing so sweetly
You have won my heart completely.
Come again and sing to me
From the blooming apple tree.

———

SONG III.

MERRILY we sing for gladness
  Without one dark cloud of sadness.
Music drives away all care
So we sing as free as air.

Merrily we sing for pleasure,
In a joyous trilling measure;
Sweet and clear the notes resound.
Here is purest pleasure found.

IV.—OUR HAPPY DAY.

OUR happy day is almost gone,
   Our songs are sung, our play is done.
The blossoms, gathered fresh with dew,
Are drooping in their places too.

But in our hearts a fairer flower
Grows sweeter with each passing hour,
Our love is steadfast, pure and bright,
Although we now must say good night.

Cho.—May He who loves the little ones
     Watch o'er us as we now shall part
And grant that in a fairer home
     Grandpa shall clasp us to his heart.

V.—THE MOCKING BIRD.

A DARLING little mocking bird
   Was singing me a song
Of all the sweetest tunes he'd heard
   Thro' all the day so long.

He sang of what the robin told
   The blue-bird and the lark,
How winter was so very cold
   And all the days were dark.

But springtime with its happy hours
    Was coming very soon
To bring back all the lovely flowers
    And happy days of June.

And so my birdie sang to me,
    From out his loving breast,
The song which all the birds so free
Had taught him while at rest.

Oh, darling little mocking bird !
    He sang his song so well !
Of all the sounds I ever heard
    'Twas like a silver bell.

THE REUNION.

PRELUDE.

DEAR FRIENDS:

It is nearly two months ago that the mail one day brought the request that I should commemorate in verse the work of the W. C. T. U. at the Soldiers' Reunion last fall.

The request was soon followed by a budget in which, snugly hidden away, I found one of the badges worn by the W. C. T. U. committee during those memorable August days. It was in the first whirl of excited feeling—pride in things accomplished, hope for things to come—that the opening stanzas of the poem were, not inappropriately, I trust, dedicated to

OUR BADGE.

TODAY I feel my pulses leap
   In cadence with my heart's wild beat.
As one wakened from his sleep
   By the *reveillee* shrill yet sweet.
And eager for the coming fray,
I greet the present glorious day.
A simple knot of ribbons tied,
Red, white and blue placed side by side—
Colors for which our heroes died,
   Emblem of freedom and of right,
The symbol of our country's pride,
   Her Union and resistless might
That bore her ever conquering—

Has stirred my heart-strings till they *ring*
In measure with the thoughts that flow
Backward toward the ' long ago."
All hail our badge! the pledge of right ;
    All hail our badge! the sign of power.
All hail our badge! From Freedom's height
    We hail that grander, nobler hour
When, Freedom's last dark foeman slain,
    Our country's banner shall display
It's radiant folds without a stain,
    Unfurled where all the winds that play
About its white and crimson bars
    Are pure, untainted by the breath
Of him who slays far more than Mars,
    And—far more cruel—by a death
By which both soul and body fall.
    All hail our badge! Once more we cry,
And down, yes down, with Alcohol!
    Ring out the shout to yonder sky!
Cheer once again red, white and blue,
And to our trust let each be true!
United let us fall or stand
For God, for Home and Native Land.

———

THE REUNION.

From all the neighboring country-side,
From town and hamlet far and wide,
    They gathered here that August day :
And some were gray and bent with years,

And some were strong and bright and gay,
Though on some faces there were tears
    All mingled with the smiles they gave
    To their old comrades grand and brave
For some were only shattered wrecks
    Of the grand manhood they had known
Since he who serves his country recks
    But little of his flesh and bone.

In uniforms of faded blue
They gathered to their rendezvous
At old Camp Allen, as they did
    Some twenty years or more ago
When Lincoln called them forth to rid
    Their land of slavery's dark woe.
Around the camp fire's ruddy blaze
They told the tales of other days;
Recounted oft the dangers shared,
    Privations bitter, hardships known;
Told o'er and o'er the way they fared
    On rusty bacon and corn pone.

We welcomed them, our soldiers true
With hearts and hands and voices, too;
We welcomed them who gave their all
    For God and Home and Native Land.
Alas! That many a rebel ball
    Had thinned the ranks of that brave band!
In mem'ry of our gallant dead
Who nobly fought for right and bled,
Yielding their lives in Freedom's need

THE REUNION.

For God, for Home and Native Land
All praise, all honor be their meed,
 Who dared to die, our hero band.

—

THE PROCESSION.

Adown the street they marched along
And, as they marched, the gathered throng
Gave cheer on cheer and cheered again.
 Before them marched in proud array
Band after band of strong young men,
 Gathered in honor of the day,--
Cadets and guards—as if again
Proud War had marshalled all his host,
His pomp to show, his strength to boast;
While prancing steed and banners bright,
 The gleam of brightly polished steel
Electric in the sun's white light,
 A brilliant pageant all reveal.

And then the veterans, battle-scarred,
With faces seamed, hands brown and hard,
With tattered flags, in well-worn blue,
 With battered knapsacks, rusty guns,
Some propped on wooden pins, a few
 With empty hanging sleeves, and all
Bearing the marks of toil and care
Marched in the place of honor there.
And louder rang the deafening cheer

THE REUNION

For them than for the splendid show
That went before them,—loud and clear
    For those who vanquished Freedom's foe.

Down many a cheek tears coursed like rain
As slowly passed the veteran train;
And throbbing hearts felt o'er again
The grief, the woe, the weary pain
That long ago had crushed them when
Their heroes died. Though not in vain
They died, grief mastered pride
And ever wept "They died! They died!"
And now their comrade's marching by
    Stirred from the lethargy of years
The slumbering grief, to wake and cry
    And spend itself in bitter tears.

Then peace with all her busy crew
Triumphant brought her trophies too;
    Here tapestries of rich design,
There spade and plow and rake and hoe,
    Here boots and shoes, there fabrics fine.
And more besides,—a goodly show.
And what came next? Our deadliest foe!
Enthroned and canopied to go,
Borne like some tyrant king of old,
    To mock our triumph, taunt our pride.
To waste our strength and steal our gold,
    To scatter ruin far and wide.

Surrounded by his minions base
There he defied us to our face;

THE REUNION.

Fluttered his banners in the air,
  Libations poured of foaming beer
In Satan's honor; Boldly there,
  Upon his face a vicious leer,
He rode—embodiment of evil, all
That devils are—King Alcohol.
Full many a victim wore his chain ;
  E'en some who conquered slavery
Were marked by his foul black'ning stain,
  The stamp of shame and misery.

And so the long line passed along
Amid the vast and surging throng
That lined the roadside, wild to view
  Their soldier heroes as they marched
Down to the camp-ground, tramping through
  The streets, all dusty, dry and parched,
Of Kekionga's olden site ;
Where myriad tents of snowy white
  Gleamed near St. Mary's flowing tide
They went, in all the pomp of might,
  Down to the pleasant riverside.

—

OUR VICTORY.

But as the martial host went down,
Out from the crowded dusty town,
One haughty rider turned him back ;
  Alone, like some grim vanquished king,
Wended along the beaten track,

Back to his stronghold hastening.
With sneer and jeer and bravado
As if defeat had galled him so
He fain would turn it all to jest,
    Back to his own dark gloomy hall,
Back with a sadly drooping crest,
    Back with his slaves came Alcohol.

For round that camp there stood a guard,
Vigilant, keeping watch and ward
Over the souls of those who slept
    Sheltered beneath the tents that night:
A band of women nobly kept
    Guard, and their watchword was
        "The Right."
Ah, yes! The right of strength and health,
The right of happiness and wealth,
Of "Peace on Earth, Good Will to Men,"
    Of joy in Heaven around the throne;
The angels echoed it again
    "Right shall henceforth on Earth be
        known."

Within their charmed circle there
Not even Alcohol might dare;
For Temperance Fair stood joined with Right
    For God, for Home and Native Land.
And sure it was a pleasant sight
    To look upon—that gentle band.
Wearing a *higher* Freedom's badge,
Linked by the holy Temperance pledge,
Bearing sweet flowers and kindly words,

Forth through the mighty host they went,
Free as the swift-winged wildwood birds,
   On their great mission all intent.

No glittering shield was theirs to wear
And never weapon did they bear.
The simple knot of ribbon gave
   Protection throughout all the field,
And those whom they had come to save
   Rev'rence by word and act revealed.
And oh, the triumph of that hour!
Freed for the time from Evil's power,
"Tenting upon the old camp ground"
   Our gallant soldiers revelled there,
And oft there rose the martial sound
   Of old war songs that filled the air.

But throughout all the merry crowd,
Though often laughter rose aloud,
Never was heard the maudlin song;
   All with one spirit seemed imbued
And Temperance ruled the mighty throng.
Long will we hail the victory grand
For God, for Home, for Native Land
Gained on the old camp ground that day.
   Long will our fainting pulses thrill
At the rememb'rance of the way
   The women worked their noble will.

Long will the thanks they gave us cheer
Us in our long hard struggle here!
Long will we hope for greater things!

As we did conquer so we may;
With this bright mem'ry fresh hope springs
    That soon shall dawn that Grander Day
When, free from Alcoholic thrall,
No more before such power to fall,
Acknowledging the sovereign sway
    Of Temperance fair, our men shall stand
In *moral freedom;*—this we pray,
    Oh God, for Home and Native Land.

———

CONCLUSION.

Let us rally round the badge, friends, rally
        once again !
Shouting the Temperance cry of Freedom !
We will swell the lofty strain, till the skies
        shall ring again,
    Shouting the Temperance cry of Freedom.

CHORUS—

For Freedom forever, be brave, friends, be brave,
Death to Alcohol !   Who'd be his slave?
Yes we'll rally round our badge, friends, rally
        once again,
    Shouting the Temperance cry of Freedom.

Oh, we'll rally here with you, round the dear
        "red, white and blue,"
    Shouting the Temperance cry of Freedom !

We have bound our ribbon white with our
    country's colors bright,
  Shouting the Temperance cry of Freedom.

We will banish shame and woe with our last
    and deadliest foe,
  Shouting the Temperance cry of Freedom!
And together we will stand for God, Home and
    Native Land,
  Shouting the Temperance cry of Freedom.

—

[Read at the Indiana State Convention, W. C. T. U., 1885, in
memory of the work done by the Fort Wayne W. C. T. U. the preced
ng fall at the Soldiers' Reunion.]

www.ingramcontent.com/pod-product-compliance
Lightning Source LLC
Chambersburg PA
CBHW030904260626
47169CB00008B/2675